Teddy and Rabbit's
Picnic Outing

Mark Burgess

First published in hardback and in Collins Toddler in
Great Britain by HarperCollins Publishers Ltd in 1995.
First published in Picture Lions in 1999.

1 3 5 7 9 10 8 6 4 2

ISBN 0 00 664696-4

Picture Lions is an imprint of the Children's Division,
part of HarperCollins Publishers Ltd.

Text and illustrations copyright © Mark Burgess 1995.

The author asserts the moral right to be identified
as the author of the work.

Printed and bound by Imago.

Teddy and Rabbit's
Picnic Outing

Mark Burgess

Picture Lions
An Imprint of HarperCollinsPublishers

Teddy and Rabbit were getting
ready for Crocodile's picnic when
Penguin came into the shop.
He was looking rather fed up.

"What's the matter, Penguin?"
asked Rabbit.

"I don't know," said Penguin.

"Cheer up!" said Teddy. "We're all invited to Crocodile's picnic and look what a lovely sunny day it is."

"I don't care about picnics
or sunny days," said Penguin.

"I'll do a little dance for you,"
said Rabbit. "Perhaps that
will cheer you up."

"It might," said Penguin.

Rabbit danced for Penguin.

"I'm a bit out of practice," she said, but Penguin didn't look quite so unhappy.

Mouse came into the shop.

"Why Penguin, you look sad," said Mouse. "What's the matter?"

"He doesn't know," said Rabbit.

"That's right," said Penguin. "I don't know."

"Magic tricks are good for cheering people up," said Mouse. "Let me show you one."

Mouse's trick went a bit wrong
but Penguin smiled all the same,
just a tiny bit.

Elephant came into the shop.

"Hello," said Elephant.

"Penguin is feeling sad," said Mouse. "We're trying to cheer him up."

"Jokes are good for cheering people up," said Elephant. "Let me tell you one."

Elephant
began
to tell
his joke...

but he couldn't
remember how it
went.

"Oh dear," said Elephant. "I'm sorry."
But Penguin laughed all the same,
rather a lot.

Crocodile came into the shop.
"So here you all are," she said. "I've
been looking for you everywhere."

"Penguin was feeling sad," said Elephant. "We've been cheering him up."

"That's right," said Penguin, "but I'm all right now."

"Good," said Crocodile. "Then let's go for our picnic."

"Yes, let's!" said Penguin.